The Magic Seed

Debbie Newhouse

All profits from this title are donated to educational nonprofits and schools. What you share keeps on sharing, and thanks!

SUMMARY: A boy and girl discover a magic seed and learn its secret which changes the lives of everyone around them.
ISBN-10: 1466398094 ISBN-13: 978-1466398092

Printed in the United States of America

For Grandma
Miriam G. Schulman
101 years old
You are my sunshine

In a town not too far away,
Two kids will begin an unusual day.

They open their front door
And see something
that wasn't there before.

A small purple box
that says "Magic Seed".
The box has instructions
which Sister can read.

THIS MAGIC SEED
IS VERY RARE.
ONLY PLANT IT
IF YOU DARE!
ALL IT GIVES YOU
YOU MUST SHARE.

The kids think, "What should
we do with this seed?"

"It might only grow up to be a weed."

If the seed came to you,
what would you do?

Luckily for you and me reading today
Those kids plant the seed right away.

And right away the seed starts to sprout!
It's fifty feet tall without a doubt!

The sister and brother begin to stare
Because it keeps shooting up higher
from there!

UP UP! Higher and higher!

Huge green leaves grow into the sky
You can't see the top even if you try!

And just then, that huge tree, like a tower,
Stops growing and starts to flower.
From every branch, leaf, and twig
Purple polka dot flowers spread out big.

Then dozens of buzzing bees come by
The bees are all smiling...
do you know why?

It's those purple flowers!
Ten thousand at least!
Those big yummy flowers
Make a huge feast!

Each bee fills up its tummy
And hurries home to make itself honey.

The flowers right then start to change,
And what comes next
is really quite strange.

That seed grows a very rare tree.
A tree called a Plumnanaberry.

Brother and Sister can't believe their eyes
The tree grows fruit that is giant in size!
Plums, pears, bananas, and berries!
Coconuts, pineapples, kumquats, and cherries!

But how could they get up so high
To taste the fruit that's in the sky?

Just then they make a discovery
In back of the Plumnanaberry.

It's an elevator door
To go up to the top floor!

The bumpy ride takes them
all the way high.
When the doors open
they can touch the sky!

SKY

They spend hours up there
chomping on treats!
If you were there,
which fruit would you eat?

They pick some fruit to take along.
As they ride down, they sing a song.

Plumnanaberry tree!
Plumnanaberry tree!
Plum
  nana
    nana
      nana
        nana
          nana
            berry
              tree!

The tree grows high
Up to the sky!
You can't see the top
Even if you try!

Do you know how it feels
To have a huge mound of fruit?
Pounds upon pounds of juicy sweet loot?

They have more fruit than
They can eat in a year!
That very fact makes them grin ear to ear!

The next morning they wake
And what do they see?
Something has happened
To the fruit from the tree!

The fruit that they kept
Has become a bit old.
It smells rather rancid
And has white wisps of mold.

Well something is wrong.
All that fruit's going bad!
What once was so fun
Now makes them feel sad.

And then they remember
about the note!
That seed has instructions that
someone wrote!

THIS MAGIC SEED
IS VERY RARE.
ONLY PLANT IT
IF YOU DARE!
ALL IT GIVES YOU
YOU MUST SHARE.

The boy and the girl
Their eyes open wide!
Share? All the fruit?
Give away their big prize?

They sit. And they listen.
A baby cries next door.

They sit. And they shiver.
It feels colder than before.

They sit. And they grumble.
The stink is hard to ignore.

They decide they must share
The fruit they adore.
They head back to the tree
To get down some more.

They ride up to the top
And bring down a fresh crop.
They set up a small shop
And put up a sign
To make people stop.

Free! Free Fruit! Come and see!
From a plumnanaberry!

Tons of people come by
To choose fruit to take.
Soon the fruit is all GONE!
Was giving it a mistake?

FREE!!
plumnanaberry
fruit

They went home feeling empty
They'd finished their chore.
But soon came a tap
A knock at the door!

A strawberry pie,
Just baked, piping hot,
Came as thanks
For berries that someone got!

Banana turns out to be just the trick
To stop baby from crying.
It stops her cries quick!

Sharing is really not
what they'd thought.
Sharing brings them nice things
that couldn't be bought.

Brother and Sister share fruit everyday,
Racing through town in a coconut sleigh!

But even though they give it away
It always comes back in a new special way.

Look! The people in town
Built a new place to play!

You'll feel just like you have wings
When you zing on cherry swings!

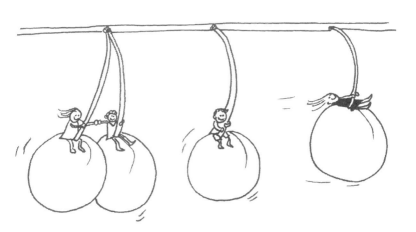

If you love playing sports,
Climb the raspberry forts!

Best of all is the watermelon pool!
It can fit all of the kids in the school!

They play at Plumnanaberry Park,
Every day until dark!

Now this seed is mysterious
And really quite rare.
But there is one secret
I simply must share.

If you want to feel joy
Like the boy and the girl
Who give magical fruit
To their town and the world...
You might not need the seed at all!

Maybe the fruit YOU have is small,

But when YOU share it,
You'll feel a thousand feet tall!

What could YOU share?
When can YOU start?

The End

but wait...

I noticed you are still here.

So am I.

Want to spend time together?

Show me what you might do...

If I had giant coconuts, plums, bananas, berries, kumquats, and cherries, I would probably make:

or maybe this instead:

and I could tell you that a kumquat is a small oval fruit like an orange with a sweet skin you can eat.

Things I Share...or Could If I Want To:

...and other things when I feel like it.

What if...

The story took place on the moon?

The tree could talk?

The elevator could go down underground?

You could live in the plumnanaberry like a giant treehouse?

Things I share sometimes:

- ☐ my ideas

- ☐ a joke

- ☐ my love

- ☐ things I don't need

- ☐ clothes that don't fit anymore

- ☐ my smile

except I also sometimes share this, too:

I know some people who are very generous.
They share a lot. Here are their names:

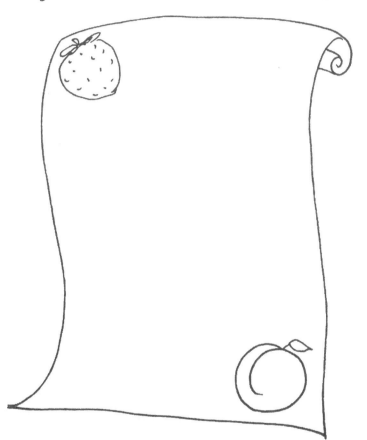

Although they never gave me
a giant coconut. Yet.

If they eat all that fruit, they will probably be very healthy. All those extra vitamins! They might also grow bigger. I think, they might grow THIS much bigger:

Regular people

People who eat Plumnanaberry fruit

The Plumnanaberry Song

Plumnanaberry tree!
Plumnanaberry tree!

Plum

   nana

      nana

        nana

           nana

              nana

                  berry tree!

The tree grows high
Up to the sky!
You can't see the top
Even if you try!

My song would go like this:

There are lots of ways The Magic Seed
story could end. Or begin.
Or be different in the middle.

So on the next few pages, I am going to
write you my own Plumnanaberry story.

My Own Plumnanaberry Story

written and illustrated by

_____

My Own Plumnanaberry Story

My Own Plumnanaberry Story

My Own Plumnanaberry Story

My Own Plumnanaberry Story

My Own Plumnanaberry Story

My Own Plumnanaberry Story

My Own Plumnanaberry Story

My Own Plumnanaberry Story

and that's the end of my story
until I think up a new one.

Actually,
I did think up another
Plumnanaberry story.
Or skit.

Or song.

Or cartoon.

Or game.

Here it is.

Plumnanaberry by Me

Plumnanaberry by Me

Plumnanaberry by Me

Plumnanaberry by Me

Plumnanaberry by Me

Plumnanaberry by Me

Plumnanaberry by Me

well, that's the end.
Thanks for reading it, too.

Bye for now.

See you in my next book.

I hope to read a book by you someday, too.

Your friend,
Debbie Newhouse

Acknowledgements

I'd like to thank many people for their encouragement and inspiration as I wrote this story.

Roughly in order of appearance, these wonderful people start with my parents, Professors John and Benita Katzenellenbogen, who gave me the gift of a maiden name that engages the imagination across all 16 letters, and their endearing parenting and love.

Jackie Ziff and Jan Bengtson, teachers who nurtured my joys and successes in reading and writing, and who told me in 8th grade, "Can't wait to see you in print."

My loving husband, Eric, who heard this story develop over several years and contributed his enthusiastic editorial and sociological insights.

My children, Laker and Lia Newhouse, who invented this tale gleefully with me driving to summer camp, and who continue to contribute illustration and plot ideas.

Early readers and editors, Kimberly Eng Lee, Meg Newhouse, Alice Carey, Larry Schwimmer, Judybeth Tropp, and Jared Curhan, whose perspectives helped improve the poetry and interactivity of the messages.

Young readers and their parents, Arthur and Sydney Mansavage, Samantha and Melanie Schwimmer, Holly and Laurel Kane, and Natalie and Julia Schillings, who inspired me with their buoyant ideas.

Enthusiasts Samantha and Stephanie Lee, and Hinako and Haruko Shimono, who bounded away from the reading to invent the Plumnanaberry song then sing it for 30 minutes straight.

Teachers at The Wetlands, Ms. Julianne, Ms. Nina, Ms. Diane, and Ms. Christina, and Lucille M. Nixon Elementary School teachers Alison Poritzky and Jodie Harrier, who welcomed me in their classrooms as an author.

Vicki Lin, Erika Grouell, and Suz Burroughs for taking delight in my creativity.

Educational pioneer and friend Kunal Chawla, who was inspired by this tale and developed a Hindi version of this story with me.

Friends Daryl Oakes, Danielle Fenton, John Vilandre, Helen Bornales, and Pam Scott who encouraged my ventures, and my uncle, Dr. Joseph D. Schulman, for getting into print and sharing suggestions on the process.

Sophia Mah, author "big sister", who shared tips and praised my budding cartoons, and Sean D'Souza whose cartooning course helped bring out my style through intensive practice.

And, my friend and colleague Matt Severson, President of The School Fund (theschoolfund.org), whose exquisite example of sharing inspired the completion of this book.

To all of you, and those others I've missed, thank you so much, and I hope you love the book.

Into books early

Debbie today

About the Author

DEBBIE NEWHOUSE is beloved as a charming entertainer who takes complicated messages and turns them into memorable stories.

She lives with her insightful husband, Eric, and two children in California. Their daughter, Lia, and son, Laker, act as eager publicists, sous-illustrators, and imagination coaches.

Readers are encouraged to write to Debbie at debbie.newhouse@gmail.com

Made in the USA
Lexington, KY
12 November 2012